This Little Tiger book belongs to:

_____

_____

_____

For all at Holy Family School, Southampton
M C

For Carrie Rose
G W

LITTLE TIGER PRESS LTD,
an imprint of the Little Tiger Group
1 Coda Studios, 189 Munster Road,
London SW6 6AW
www.littletiger.co.uk

First published in Great Britain 1998
This edition published 2014

Printed in China • LTP/1800/3242/0320

2 4 6 8 10 9 7 5 3

One, Two, Three, Oops!

Michael Coleman
Gwyneth Williamson

LITTLE TIGER
LONDON

Mr. and Mrs. Rabbit had a big family . . .

A *very* big family . . .

A very, *very* big family!

"I wonder how many babies we have?"
said Mr. Rabbit one morning. "I think I'll
count them."

"Why not wait until later?" said Mrs. Rabbit.
"I would."

"No," said Mr. Rabbit firmly. "I'll do it now."

So he went outside to where the babies
were playing. Mr. Rabbit started counting.
"One, two, three . . . oops! Oh, noggin-
sploggin!" he exclaimed.

With a hop and a skip, the babies he'd
counted ran off to join their brothers
and sisters. He couldn't tell which ones
he'd counted and which he hadn't.

Mr. Rabbit started again. This time he got
a little further. "One, two, three, four . . . oops!
Oh, noggin-sploggin, boodle-doodle!" he
grumbled.

The babies had started a game of tag
and moved. He'd lost count again.

Mr. Rabbit tried one more time.
"One, two, three, four, five . . . oops!
Oh, noggin-sploggin, boodle-doodle,
grizzly-wizzly!" he groaned.

The babies had started playing hide-and-seek.
Now he couldn't see any of them. He'd lost
count again.

"This is no good," said Mr. Rabbit. "I'll have
to think of a better way."

So he sat and thought . . . until he had a good idea. "I know," he said. "I'll give a carrot to every baby I count. That way I'll see the ones I've missed."

So Mr. Rabbit started counting again. This time he gave a carrot to each baby he counted. "One, two, three, four, five, six . . . oops! Oh, noggin-sploggin, boodle-doodle, grizzly-wizzly, sniffy-whiffy!" he cried.

The babies he'd
given carrots to
had eaten them!
He couldn't tell
who he'd counted
and who he hadn't.

"I know," said Mr. Rabbit,
as he had another good idea.
"I'll tell them to sit down
when I've counted them.
That way I won't get
mixed up."

So Mr. Rabbit told his babies to sit down once he'd counted them. "One, two, three, four, five, six, seven . . . oops! Oh, noggin-sploggin, boodle-doodle, grizzly-wizzly, sniffy-whiffy, jingle-bingle!" he shouted.

The ground was full of prickly weeds. Just as soon
as a baby sat down, it jumped up again! Mr. Rabbit
had lost count once more!

"Right, this will definitely work," said Mr. Rabbit,
as he had yet another idea. "I'll send every baby
indoors. The ones still outside will be the ones
I haven't counted. I can't possibly get confused
that way!"

So Mr. Rabbit started counting again. This time, every baby he counted was sent indoors.

"One, two, three, four, five, six, seven, eight . . . oops! Oh, noggin-sploggin, boodle-doodle, grizzly-wizzly, sniffy-whiffy, jingle-bingle, fuddle-duddle!" yelled Mr. Rabbit, stamping his foot.

He'd forgotten that their home had
a back door. Every baby he'd sent in
the front had run straight out the back.
He'd lost count yet again.

Mr. Rabbit sat down and thought once more. He thought all afternoon . . .

and he thought all evening. And then he noticed a patch of mud on the ground and had his best idea yet.

"I've got it!" said Mr. Rabbit. "Every time
I count a baby I'll put mud on its tail.
Then I'll know that the babies with clean
tails are the ones I haven't counted. It can't
possibly go wrong!"

So Mr. Rabbit began to count once more.
Every time he counted a baby, he put a
blob of mud on its tail. "One, two, three,
four, five, six, seven, eight, nine . . . oops!
Oh, noggin-sploggin, boodle-doodle,
grizzly-wizzly, sniffy-whiffy, jingle-bingle,
fuddle-duddle, jungle-bungle!"
he roared, jumping up
and down . . .

It had started to rain.
All the blobs of mud
he'd put on the babies
he'd counted had been
washed off. He'd lost
count yet again!

"I give up!" said Mr. Rabbit. He stomped angrily back indoors. "I don't know how to count those babies!" he cried. "I'm fed up!"

At that moment Mr. and Mrs. Rabbit's babies
scampered back indoors. Tired and happy after
playing all day they were soon fast asleep.
"I told you to wait until later," said Mrs. Rabbit.
"Now try counting them."

Mr. Rabbit began counting once again.
"One, two, three, four, five, six, seven,
eight, nine, TEN!" he cried. "I've done it!"
"Oh no you haven't," said Mrs. Rabbit . . .

"What about the littlest ones?"